Tight Squeeze

With a sickening dull *pop,* Tooms dislocated his left shoulder from the socket. His shoulder slipped down into the opening. There was another *pop,* and the right shoulder followed. Tooms could smell Thomas Werner's sweat. Feel the heat of the blood in his veins. With every sense focused on his victim, what he had to do next was easy. Drawing on his incredible strength, Tooms began to squeeze himself down the narrow chimney.

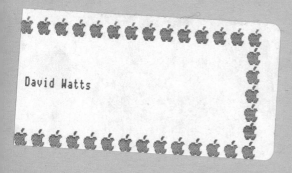

David Watts

THE ⊗ FILES™

SQUEEZE

a novel by Ellen Steiber

based on the television series
The X-Files created by Chris Carter
based on the teleplay
written by Glen Morgan and James Wong

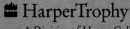 HarperTrophy
A Division of HarperCollinsPublishers

To Mimi Panitch, Terri Windling,
and Tania Yatskievych,
intrepid traveling companions and good friends

SQUEEZE

Chapter ONE

Seven thirty. As the last of a bloodred sunset streaked the Baltimore sky, throngs of working people crowded the streets, hurrying to get home before darkness fell.

All except George Usher, a middle-aged businessman. He was heading back to his office for a long evening of work. And he was less than happy about it.

As he left the elevator and stepped onto the fifteenth floor of his office building, Usher sighed. Empty cubicles. Long, silent hallways, lit here and there with Exit signs that glowed eerily in the dim, gray after-hours lights.

The office felt different at night. Creepy. *Excellent security,* Usher reminded himself. *No one can get in unless they work here.* But it still felt strange.

Usher walked into his office, turned on the light, and punched a number into his phone. An answering machine clicked on, and his wife's voice asked callers to leave a message after the beep.

"Hello, honey," he said. "It's about seven thirty and it looks like I'll be here awhile. The meeting didn't go so well. Call me. I love you. 'Bye."

Usher hung up and stared into the dark hallway outside his office. Suddenly he felt an odd tremor. Fear.

Coffee, he thought. *A cup of coffee will help.* He grabbed his mug and headed for the coffee machine at the other end of the floor, making his way down a long row of empty offices.

His office, however, was not empty.

The instant he left it, a tiny noise broke the silence. High on the wall across from Usher's desk, the cover of an air vent moved, ever so slightly. The two screws holding the vent in place began to turn. First the right. Then the left. Then, very slowly, long, slender fingertips reached out from inside the vent, pushing the cover aside.

Usher started back down the hallway, his mug filled with day-old coffee. He stopped short as he reached his office door. He could have sworn he'd left the light on inside.

He stepped into the dark office, groping for the lamp on his desk. Then the door slammed shut with an unearthly force. And Usher suddenly knew that he wasn't alone.

Frantically he reached for the door. He got hold of the knob and fought to open it. But someone—or something—had hold of him.

Usher was desperate. He struggled in the

stranger's grasp and slipped free. He rolled across the desk—only to feel powerful hands lock around his throat. He couldn't breathe. He couldn't make a sound as his body was lifted into the air with inhuman strength.

For a brief moment the hands left his throat. Usher's pitiful scream rang through the office as his body slammed into the door with enough force to splinter it.

And then there was only silence.

An hour later George Usher's office was blanketed in cold, white moonlight. Coffee from his overturned mug dripped onto the carpet, which was already soaked with blood. His lifeless body lay a short distance away.

Directly above the body, one of the screws in the cover of the air vent began to turn. Something inside the vent was screwing the cover back into the wall. Slowly. Victoriously.

Chapter TWO

Sunlight streamed though the windows of a building in downtown Washington, D.C. In the open court of an atrium, F.B.I. Special Agent Dana Scully was having lunch with Tom Colton.

For Scully this was a relaxing break in a hectic day. The atrium restaurant was one of her favorites. And Tom was an old friend. They'd attended Quantico, the F.B.I. training academy, together.

It had been a while since the two agents had seen each other. Colton looked exactly the way she remembered him: handsome, intelligent, and self-assured. He'd always liked loud ties, and the one he wore today was no exception—black with big white polka dots. And he still spoke in a low, rapid voice that made everything sound urgent. But right now Colton was just catching Scully up on gossip.

"Guess who I ran into from our class at Quantico." he said. "Marty Neil."

Scully laughed. "J. Edgar Junior?" she said. J. Edgar Hoover had been the director of the F.B.I. for almost fifty years, until 1972. Marty Neil, their classmate, planned to have a career just like Hoover's. The problem was, Neil wasn't nearly as smart as Hoover had been. But he was every bit as paranoid.

"Neil just got bumped up," Colton told Scully. "He's going to work for Foreign Counterintelligence. New York City Bureau. *Supervisory* special agent."

"Supervisory?" Scully echoed in surprise. "He's only been out of the academy for two years. How did he land that?"

Colton gave her a wry smile. "He lucked into the World Trade Center bombing. A major crime that was solved. Quickly."

"Well, good for Marty," Scully said, shaking off a slight feeling of envy. Lately her own career didn't seem nearly as promising. Scully had an undergraduate degree in astronomy, a medical degree, and an advanced degree in physics. It was while she was getting her physics degree that she'd joined the F.B.I. She'd done well at Quantico, so well that she had been asked to teach there. And that was when she'd gotten her current assignment. Section Chief Bevins had paired her with Fox Mulder, an agent who specialized in investigating cases no one else would touch.

"C'mon, Dana." Colton's voice snapped her out of her thoughts. "Marty Neil's a loser. But look where he is now. It's where *we* should be."

Scully studied her former classmate. She knew Colton wasn't doing as badly as he made it sound. "Brad Wilson told me that the work you did on the Washington Crossing killer led them right to the suspect," she said. "The word is, you're on the Violent Crimes Section's fast track."

Colton shrugged, as if that wasn't a big deal. But Scully knew he was pleased with his reputation. Colton had always been ambitious. Getting ahead fast meant everything to him.

"How've you been doing?" Colton asked. "Had any close encounters of the third kind?"

Scully tried not to let the remark bother her. She knew he was kidding. Besides, she couldn't really blame him for thinking her assignment was strange. It *was.* "Is that what everyone thinks I do?" she asked carefully. "Have close encounters?"

"No, no, of course not," Colton protested. "But you do work with 'Spooky' Mulder."

Scully's partner, Fox Mulder, was known as an excellent agent. He had graduated from Harvard and Oxford with honors in psychology. He also happened to have a photographic memory. Scully had never met anyone who was sharper when it came to analyzing a case. But Mulder was even better known for his interest in unexplained phenomena. He actually believed in things like UFOs and aliens. And he'd dedicated his life to investigating them.

"Mulder's ideas may be a bit 'out there,'" Scully admitted. "But he's a great agent."

Colton took a bite of his lunch and sighed. "Well, I've got a case that's 'out there,'" he said, his voice troubled. "The Baltimore Police Department wants our help on a serial killer profile. Three murders. Began six weeks ago. The victims vary in age, gender, and race. No known connections to each other."

Scully sipped her iced tea. "I take it there's a pattern?" she asked.

"The killer's point of entry," Colton answered. "Actually, the lack of one."

"What do you mean?" Scully asked.

"One victim," Colton began, "was a college girl. She was killed in her ten-foot-by-twelve-foot cinder-block dorm room. When she was found, the windows were locked and the door was chained *from the inside*. No one can figure how the killer got in. And then out again."

Scully listened intently as Colton continued. "The last incident was two days ago. High-security office building. Nothing on the security monitors out of the ordinary. It was after-hours. Everyone had gone home. The guy parked in the garage, took the elevator to the fifteenth floor. He was going back to his office for an evening of work. No one else came into the building. The guy never came out."

"Could they be suicides?" Scully asked.

Colton shook his head. Carefully he removed a photograph from his briefcase and handed it to Scully.

Scully's eyes widened when she saw the picture taken at the crime scene.

"The victims' livers have been removed," Colton said. "Without tools."

"You mean the murderer used his bare hands?" Scully asked in disbelief. Her mind searched for a rational explanation. "There had to be a knife or scalpel—"

Colton cut her off with a shake of his head. "I know it sounds impossible, but no. There was no cutting tool. I can't even begin to guess how he did it."

"This sounds like an X-file," Scully said. An "X-file" was what the F.B.I. called a case that involved strange happenings and unexplained phenomena. The X-files were Fox Mulder's specialty.

"Let's not get carried away," Colton warned her. "I'm the one who's going to solve these murders. I'm not handing them over to you and Mulder. But what I'd like you to do is go over the case histories. Come down to the crime scene. It's only a half hour from your house."

Scully looked at him quizzically. "If you're going to solve the case, then why do you want me in on it?"

Colton didn't meet her eyes as he answered. "Maybe because of the cases you've been stuck with lately—you'll have a fresh angle."

Scully took this in. Colton thought there was something crazy about working on the X-files. He was also making sure that just in case it *wasn't* crazy, he'd have her expertise. But if he really wanted someone with X-file experience, he'd need her partner as well.

"You want me to ask Mulder to help?" Scully asked.

Colton frowned. "If Mulder wants to come and do you a favor, great," he said. "But make sure he knows this is *my* case."

Scully examined the photo again. She was sure the case was an X-file.

"Dana," Colton said. "If I can break a case like this one . . . *I'll* be getting the bump up the ladder. And you . . ."

Scully looked at him. "What about me?"

Colton glanced away as he answered. "They'll stop calling you Mrs. Spooky."

Scully sat absolutely still as Colton picked up the check and left the table. That last remark had hurt. And Colton, of course, had known that it would.

Chapter THREE

The next morning Scully did as Colton had asked. Instead of going straight to F.B.I. headquarters, she stopped at George Usher's office building and parked in the garage below the skyscraper. She glanced at the television monitors suspended from the ceiling. It was definitely a high-security building.

It was still early, just after seven. Scully stepped off the elevator onto the fifteenth floor. The office was deserted—except for one person. Fox Mulder. Scully had thought long and hard after her lunch with Colton, and she'd decided to tell Mulder about this case. It sounded too much like an X-file to leave him out.

Now Mulder stood in Usher's office. His forensic kit was spread out. He'd taken off his jacket, and his sleeves were rolled up. He wore a latex glove on one hand. He'd been at work for a while.

"Morning," he said to Scully.

Fox Mulder looked surprisingly young for an agent with so much experience. He was a tall, slender man who wore his hair longer than was common for an F.B.I. agent. Scully thought there was some-thing a little deceptive about Mulder's appearance. His face seemed so innocent, almost boyish. Until you looked into his clear hazel eyes. That was when you realized that Fox Mulder had seen more than most people. And it had cost him.

Scully nodded at Mulder. She was glad Colton wasn't here yet. That gave her a chance to make her own notes on the crime scene. She surveyed the office with a practiced eye.

Usher's body had been removed, but the office was still a wreck. The top of Usher's desk looked as if it had been through a storm. Pens, pencils, and folders lay scattered. A picture of a woman, proba-bly his wife, had been knocked over. So had the desk lamp and a coffee mug.

And blood was splattered everywhere—across the papers on Usher's desk, on his chair, on the rug, on the walls.

There was only one orderly area in the office—the corner where Mulder had spread out his foren-sic kit. Fingerprint powder, razors, and tweezers were all neatly arranged.

Mulder, too, scanned the bloody office. Then his eyes came back to his partner.

"So . . . why didn't they ask me?" he asked Scully.

Scully was quiet. Mulder waited patiently for an

answer. He reached into his pocket for a sunflower seed.

"They're friends of mine from the Academy," Scully said at last. She was trying to be tactful. "I'm sure they just felt more comfortable talking to me."

"Why would I make them so uncomfortable?" Mulder asked.

Scully faced him, hesitating. Then, as usual, she decided that the best answer was an honest one. "It's probably because of your . . . reputation."

"Reputation?" he echoed, sounding puzzled. "*I* have a reputation?"

Mulder was deliberately giving her a hard time, and Scully knew it. "Look," she said impatiently. "Colton plays by the book, and you don't. They feel your methods, your theories are . . ."

"Spooky?" Mulder guessed. His smile was amused, but his eyes were serious as he asked, "What about you? You think I'm . . . spooky?"

Scully paused, wondering whether Mulder deserved a straight answer. She knew he was testing her. They'd been working together only a short time. And Mulder knew that, originally, Scully had been assigned to spy on him. To give the F.B.I. a reason to shut down the X-files. But Scully had an open mind. Although she didn't always agree with Mulder's theories, she respected his methods. She'd told her supervisors the truth: that Mulder was an excellent agent. That the cases he investigated were real. By now, she thought, Mulder ought to trust her.

Scully never answered Mulder's question. Because at that moment Tom Colton strode into the room.

"Dana, I'm sorry I'm late," he said.

"No problem. We just got here," Scully told him. "This is Fox Mulder. Mulder, Tom Colton." The two men shook hands.

"So, Mulder." Colton spoke in a mocking tone. "What do you think? This look like the work of Little Green Men?"

Scully shot Mulder a sympathetic glance.

"Gray," Mulder replied seriously.

"What?" Colton asked.

"Gray," Mulder explained. "You said 'Green Men.' A Reticulian's skin tone is gray. They're known for their extraction of human livers due to a lack of iron in the Reticulian galaxy."

Scully wished Mulder wouldn't do this. Even if Colton deserved it. She knew Colton was already prejudiced against Mulder. And now Mulder was making it worse.

Colton looked confused—as though he couldn't tell whether Mulder was joking. "You can't be serious," he said.

"Do you know how much liver and onions go for on Reticulum?" Mulder asked Colton. Then, before Colton could answer, he excused himself and continued examining the office.

Colton's face flushed red with embarrassment. He scowled at Mulder, then moved off to the other side of the room. Scully sighed and followed Colton. Maybe it wasn't too late to smooth things out between the two agents.

Mulder paid no attention to Colton and Scully's conversation. He continued his investigation of Usher's office, searching the sharp corners on the desk for any fibers that might have pulled loose from the murderer's clothes.

Reaching into his pocket for more sunflower seeds, Mulder moved on to the window. Carefully he checked for points of entry. He wasn't surprised when he didn't find any. Next he made his way along the edges of the room. He was looking for anything the murderer might have dropped or touched. Any bit of evidence that might lead them to a suspect.

Mulder stopped as he saw something glittering in the carpet. Kneeling down, he gently pressed the carpet with his index finger. There *was* something—tiny metal filings.

Using tweezers, Mulder lifted a filing and held it up to the light. He thought for a second, then gazed up. High above him on the wall was the metal grille that covered the office's air vent.

Mulder stood up and went straight to his forensic kit. He grabbed the fingerprint powder, fingerprint tape, and brush. He rolled the brush handle rapidly between his hands to clean the bristles. Then he began to lightly powder the area around the vent.

This caught Colton's attention. "What the hell is he doing?" he asked Scully in a suspicious tone.

Mulder paid him no attention. He was focused on the brush, hoping to lift a clean print.

Colton watched in disbelief. "That's a one-foot-square vent," he told Mulder. "And even if a Reticulian could crawl through, the vent cover is screwed in place."

Mulder ignored Colton and continued to stroke the fingerprint brush along the sides of the grille. Bit by bit, a print was emerging. It was long and thin. It had some of the qualities of a human fingerprint, but it was definitely *not* human.

Mulder didn't say a word. But his eyes went wide with amazement. He'd seen these prints before.

Chapter FOUR

Scully drew up a chair beside Mulder. They were in Mulder's cramped office, in the basement of F.B.I. headquarters. As usual, the tiny room was overflowing with stacks of books and papers. Mulder's bulletin board was covered with photos of blurred objects. Maybe they were UFOs, maybe not. Scully wasn't sure. But Mulder's attitude toward his work was clear from the poster on his wall, which read I WANT TO BELIEVE.

Scully ignored a mountain of reports that was threatening to topple onto the floor. She focused her attention on the slides Mulder was showing her. There were six, and she wasn't sure what to make of them. Each showed an elongated fingerprint. The prints were definitely too long and thin to be human.

Mulder pointed to one of the slides. "This is the print I took yesterday from Usher's office," he said. "These others are from the X-files."

"How many murders are we talking about?" Scully asked in surprise.

"Eleven, counting Usher," Mulder answered.

"Ten murders before him. All in the Baltimore area. No point of entry in any of them. Each victim was murdered the same way. These prints"—he lined up five slides—"were from five of those other ten crime scenes."

"*Ten* other murders?" Scully still couldn't believe it. "Colton never mentioned—"

"I don't think he's even aware of them," Mulder said. He pointed to three of the slides. "These three prints were lifted in 1963, five years before Colton was even born. And these two were taken in 1933."

Scully's eyes widened. "You're saying the same murderer was at work thirty years ago *and* sixty years ago?"

"And ninety," Muller said. "Unfortunately, we don't have prints for that one. Fingerprinting wasn't too common in 1903. And police records weren't very complete. But there *was* at least one similar murder then."

"Of course," Scully said dryly. She pushed her chair away from the desk. *Leave it to Mulder*, she thought, *to come up with a completely unbelievable case history*.

Mulder ignored her tone and began adding up the evidence. "Five murders, every thirty years. That means he's got two more to go this year."

Scully stood up and turned away from her partner. *There has to be a more logical explanation*, she told herself. She was a scientist, a doctor. There was no way she could believe— She stopped herself. Maybe she'd misunderstood Mulder.

"You're saying these are copycat crimes?" she asked. "Someone who knows about the old crimes and is determined to copy their pattern?"

Mulder spun his chair around to face her. "What did we learn on our first day at the Academy, Scully?" he asked in a mock-stern voice. *"Every fingerprint is unique.* These are all a perfect match."

Scully took this in. She knew exactly what Mulder was driving at. It was one thing for him to have weird ideas. It was another for him to expect *her* to believe them. "Are you suggesting I go to the Violent Crimes Section and tell them these murders were done by . . . an alien?" she asked.

"Of course not," Mulder replied, deadpan. "I find no evidence of alien involvement."

Scully glared at him. "What then?" she asked. "That this is the work of a hundred-year-old serial killer, capable of overpowering a healthy six-foot-two businessman?"

Mulder grinned at her. "And he should really stick out in a crowd, with ten-inch fingers."

"Mulder, if you think this is a joke—"

"The X-files investigate unsolved cases involving

unexplained phenomena," Mulder reminded her. "This should be our case. And I'm quite serious."

"It's Colton's case," Scully told him.

Mulder handed her a yellowed file. "The X-file dates back to 1903. We had it first."

Scully sighed. She didn't want to offend Mulder. But sometimes he was so stubborn that she had no choice.

"Mulder," she said gently. "They don't want you involved. They don't want to hear your theories. That's why Section Chief Blevins has you hidden away down here in the basement."

Mulder didn't seem at all hurt by this. "You're down here too," he pointed out cheerfully.

Scully slumped in her chair. She was tired of arguing. Couldn't he ever take no for an answer?

Mulder moved to her side. "Why don't we agree to this," he suggested. "Colton and his group have their investigation. And we have ours. And never the twain shall meet. Agreed?"

Scully looked at him, unable to answer.

And unable to refuse.

The clock read 10:00 P.M. Scully sat alone in her apartment, her eyes fixed on her computer screen. Spread out on her desk were her notes from the case. She'd gone over the evidence they'd found in

Usher's office. And she'd read through Mulder's X-files. Now she was writing a profile of the killer.

Once again she considered Mulder's theory. And then she went ahead with her own.

"After a careful review of the violent and powerful nature of these murders," she wrote, "I believe the killer to be a male, twenty-five to thirty-five years of age. He has above-average intelligence. His method of entry has so far been undetectable. This may be due to his superior knowledge of the inner structure of buildings and ducts."

Scully glanced at the blueprints of Usher's office building and continued writing. "Or he may, in fact, hide in plain sight. For example, he might pose as a deliveryman or maintenance worker. Witnesses tend to overlook such personnel. Their uniforms often render them invisible to casual observers."

Once again Scully studied the slide of the elongated fingerprint. Then she put it down, feeling frustrated. She couldn't explain the strange print, and she wasn't about to try. Instead she dealt with another aspect of the murder.

"The removal of the liver is the most important detail of these crimes. The liver possesses restorative qualities. It cleanses the blood . . . ."

The next morning Scully presented her report to the Violent Crimes Section. She knew it was important to sound professional and sure of herself. She wasn't about to mention Mulder's strange theories—or her own doubts. Both Colton and his boss, Agent Fuller, were at the conference table, listening intently.

Calmly Scully explained her theory about why the murderer took his victims' livers. "The taking of this trophy may allow the killer to believe he's cleansing himself of his own impurities," she said. "I think he's acting under the classic form of obsessive-compulsive behavior."

Several of the agents nodded at this.

"Since the victims are unrelated," Scully went on, "we can't predict who will be next. So we must use the fact that serial killers don't always succeed in finding a victim. When this happens, the serial killer may return in frustration to the site of the previous murder."

"Why would he do that?" a balding agent asked.

"He'd be trying to recapture the emotional high of the last murder," Scully explained. "So I believe our best course of action is to target those sites where he's already killed."

Agent Fuller stood up. "Good job, Agent Scully," he said. Then he turned to the agents under his command. "If there are no objections, I'd like to begin our stakeouts of the murder sites tonight. We're looking for a male, twenty-five to thirty-five. He may be wearing a uniform: gas company, UPS, whatever."

Fuller turned back to Scully. "I know you're assigned to another area," he said. "But if you don't mind some overtime, you're welcome to join us. That is," he added, "if you don't mind working in an area that's a bit more down-to-earth."

Scully forced herself to smile as the other agents laughed at Fuller's lame joke. She knew Mulder wouldn't have found it funny either.

Chapter FIVE

Three days later Scully once again parked her car in the high-security garage below George Usher's office building. The Violent Crimes Section had taken her advice. Agents were conducting stakeouts at the sites of the previous murders. Scully had volunteered for this position. Now she put on a small headset and settled in to wait.

Though dusk had just fallen, the garage was deserted. Scully wondered if people were leaving work early because of Usher's murder.

"Position ten, this is a station check," said the voice in her headset.

"Position ten, I copy," Scully whispered back.

Her eyes scanned the area, sorting through the shadows. The garage was dimly lit. The silence was deafening. She began a second visual check. Nothing.

And then she heard it—footsteps.

She wasn't alone.

Slowly, quietly, Scully got out of the car. She drew her weapon. She aimed her flashlight in the direction of the sound.

The footsteps stopped. Scully shined her light along the grease-stained floor. Around the thick cement support columns. She saw nothing but the vast, empty garage.

And then she heard the footsteps again. Someone was walking quickly and deliberately. Someone was coming toward her.

Keeping her back to the wall, Scully moved toward the sound. She was getting closer. Whoever was in the garage with her was on the other side of this wall.

Scully tucked the flashlight into the waistband of her pants. She rounded the corner fast, both hands bracing her gun. She aimed it straight out in front of her—and directly at Mulder's chest.

Her partner raised his hands in surrender. "You wouldn't shoot an unarmed man, would you?" he joked.

Scully gave him a look of disgust. Then she holstered her weapon. "Mulder," she said in a fierce whisper, "what are you doing here?"

"He's not coming back here," Mulder said, ignoring her question. "Our suspect gets his thrill from the challenge of a seemingly impossible entry. He's already beaten this place. If you'd read the X-file on the case, you would have come to the same conclusion."

"You're jeopardizing my stakeout," Scully said angrily. She was working for the Violent Crimes Section now. Mulder had no right to interfere. And he had no right to tell her that her theories were wrong.

Mulder held out his hand to her, palm up. "Want some sunflower seeds?" he asked mildly.

Scully turned her back on him, steaming.

"You're wasting your time," Mulder told her. "I'm going home."

He watched as Scully returned to her car. Then he walked off into the darkness.

But Mulder didn't go home. He was too intrigued by this case to let it go. Hours later he was still walking through the shadows of the garage. Night had fallen. Except for Scully, everyone seemed to have left the office building. Mulder could hear the hum of the air-circulation pump and the whine of the building's electrical system. And then he heard a dull metallic *clang*.

Quickly Mulder took cover behind one of the support pillars. He peered out, trying to see around the corner. The sounds seemed to be coming from an area enclosed by a chain-link fence.

Curious, Mulder approached the fenced area. The sounds were definitely growing louder. The fence surrounded the large motors, encased in sheet-metal, of the building's air-circulation system. Mulder stepped back, studying the system. From here the air-circulation ducts branched upward into the office building.

He moved in with his flashlight, examining the system more closely. The clanging and banging sounds were getting louder. Definitely coming from the ducts. As if something was inside them. And a metal panel that was part of the motor casing was out of place. As if it had been opened.

Again Mulder shined his light around the area. That's when he noticed that the gate in the chain-link fence was open. Not by much. Just enough for someone to slip through. What if this was the point of entry? What if the murderer had entered the building through this duct system?

Mulder stepped through the open gate and then tensed. The ventilation duct moved. It flexed from the inside. Almost as if it were breathing.

Something was scaling the duct from inside.

Mulder took off.

"Scully!" he shouted, racing toward her car. "Call for backup and get over here!"

Scully got on the radio. "Position ten, request backup!"

Then she got out of the car and followed Mulder to the fenced-in area.

"In there," Mulder said, pointing toward the ducts.

Scully drew her gun. "Federal agent!" she shouted. "I'm armed! Don't move!"

The movement in the metal duct stopped.

"Get down . . . slowly," Scully ordered.

There was silence for a moment. Then the duct began to creak and groan as the climber inside moved downward.

Scully and Mulder waited. The duct flexed and pulsed until whoever was inside finally stopped moving.

Scully kept her gun trained on the open panel at the base of the motors. "All right, now get out!" she commanded. Her voice was firm, but her muscles were locked with tension. What was crawling through the skyscraper's duct system?

Scully felt her tension ease as she heard her backup arrive. Four more agents, including Colton, ran toward them. They too aimed their weapons at the open panel.

Scully watched intently. She could just make out a man, crouching in the darkness of the opening. He hesitated beyond the glare of the agents' flash-lights. Then he crawled out feetfirst.

He looked to be in his early twenties. He had a boyish face with a high forehead framed by short, straight bangs. He wore a tan uniform with an emblem that read ANIMAL CONTROL. His face shined with sweat. Shaking, he raised his hands over his head. He looked scared to death. Like a rabbit caught in headlights.

"Take him," Colton ordered.

The other agents moved in and handcuffed him.

"You are under arrest," one of the agents told the suspect. "You have the right to remain silent. Anything you say can and will be held against you in a court of law. . . ."

Colton turned to Scully. "Good job, Dana," he said, making sure Mulder heard him.

Scully didn't respond. She wasn't about to celebrate—not in front of Mulder, who looked shaken.

Mulder came up to Scully. "You were right," he said. "Your profile nailed him perfectly." Then he walked off without another word.

Scully watched her partner go. She *was* right. And for once Mulder was wrong. So why, she wondered, didn't that feel good?

Chapter SIX

Scully sat behind the two-way mirror. She was looking into a bleak room in the Baltimore Police headquarters. With her were Mulder, Colton, Fuller, and two police officers. They were all watching as a woman with short blond hair prepared to give a lie-detector test to the suspect.

The suspect wore fluorescent orange prison coveralls. He was sitting in a chair, facing the two-way mirror. Scully knew that though they could see him, he couldn't see them.

One of the suspect's arms was strapped down and fastened with a blood-pressure cuff. Wires ran from the machine to sensors on his fingertips.

Scully knew that his blood pressure, heart rate, and breathing rate were all about to be measured. A change in any one of them might mean that he was lying. The suspect looked the way he had that night in the garage—young and scared. Scully was curious about what would happen during the polygraph test.

The woman adjusted the machine so that the ink flowed through the stylus and the graph paper moved.

She began the test with a simple question. "Is your full name Eugene Victor Tooms?"

"Yes," the suspect answered.

"Do you live in the state of Maryland?"

"Yes," Tooms said.

"Are you employed by Baltimore Municipal Animal Control?"

"Yes," he answered again.

The examiner watched the graph paper and marked "7/+" next to the response. So far, Scully knew, the suspect was telling the truth.

"Eugene, is it your intent to lie to me about anything here today?" the woman asked.

"No," Tooms replied. He spoke in a monotone, and his eyes seemed glazed, as if he were in a trance.

"Were you ever enrolled in college?"

"Yes."

"Were you ever enrolled in medical school?"

"No."

"Have you ever removed a liver from a human being?"

"No," Tooms replied.

"Have you ever killed a living creature?"

"Yes." Like his voice, Tooms's face was completely neutral, empty of all emotion.

"Have you ever killed a human being?"

"No," he answered.

"Have you ever been in George Usher's office?" the examiner asked.

"No," Tooms answered.

"Did you kill George Usher?"

"No," he replied again.

"Are you over one hundred years old?"

Tooms hesitated, looking surprised by the question. Then he answered, "No."

On the other side of the two-way mirror, Colton was also surprised by the strange query. "That must have been a control question," he said.

"Actually," Mulder said, "I told her to ask that."

Colton gave Mulder a puzzled look, then turned his attention back to the lie-detector test.

"Have you ever been to Powhatan Mill?" the examiner asked.

"Yes," Tooms answered.

"In 1933?"

Again the suspect hesitated before saying, "No."

Colton scowled at Mulder. "You again?"

Mulder nodded, his eyes locked on Eugene Tooms.

"Are you afraid you might fail this test?" the examiner asked.

Tooms looked uncertain. Now the pressure was definitely getting to him. "Well . . . yes," he admitted. "'Cause I didn't do anything."

The examiner looked at the graph and nodded. "Thank you, Mr. Tooms. That will be all for now."

A short while later, Tooms had been returned to his cell by the police officers. Scully, Mulder, and Colton all stood in the interrogation room, waiting for the results of the test.

"Eugene Tooms nailed it," the examiner told them. "A plus. As far as I'm concerned, the subject did not kill those people."

Mulder didn't seem satisfied with this. He took the graph paper from the machine and sat down to examine it.

Agent Fuller entered the room with a sigh. "Tooms checks out," he announced. "The maintenance people in Usher's office building confirmed calling Animal Control because of a bad smell in the building. And they found a dead cat in the ventilation ducts on the second floor."

Colton stood up. "Well, that ends that."

"No, it doesn't," Scully argued. "It doesn't explain what Tooms was doing there in the middle of the night."

Fuller shrugged. "So he's one of the few civil

servants we have with dedication. And we busted him for it."

"Tooms was crawling up the air duct by himself, without alerting security," Scully reminded him.

"Dana," Colton said, "Tooms passed the test. His story checks out. He's not the guy. This doesn't mean your profile is incorrect."

"Scully's right," Mulder said. His eyes were still on the graph paper, and he spoke with total confidence. "Tooms *is* the guy."

Fuller looked at Mulder as though he'd just announced that the moon was purple. "Okay, Mulder." He spoke in the overly patient voice of a parent dealing with a troublesome child. "Whadd'ya got?"

Mulder pointed to the graph paper. "Tooms lied on questions twelve and fourteen," he explained. "These responses nearly go off the chart."

Fuller studied the graph paper with a skeptical expression. "Is number twelve the question about being a hundred years old?" he asked. "Let me tell ya, *I* had a reaction to that stupid question. And what was that Powhatan Mill thing?"

"Two murders with matching methods occurred in Powhatan Mill in 1933," Mulder answered.

The examiner cleared her throat. "My interpretation of those reactions—"

Fuller was out of patience. "I don't need you or that machine to tell me if Tooms was alive in thirty-three!" he yelled.

"He's the guy," Mulder said calmly.

Fuller glared at him. "Well, if he is, I'm letting him go!" With that the supervisor stomped out of the room. The door slammed behind him.

Slowly Colton stood up and moved toward the door. From the expression on his face, Scully knew that he agreed with Fuller. And that he didn't believe Mulder at all.

"Coming?" Colton asked Scully.

Scully hesitated. She could choose to work with the Violent Crimes Section. Or she could continue to work with Mulder.

"Tom," she began. "I . . . I want to thank you for letting me work with your section. But I'm officially assigned to the X-files."

Colton's eyes moved to Mulder, who was still looking over the charts. "I'll see what I can do about that," he said.

"Tom," Scully said at once, "I can look out for myself. And I don't want to—"

"You said Mulder was 'out there,'" Colton broke in.

Mulder glanced up at him with a look of polite interest. Scully wished she were somewhere else. Far away.

"But Mulder's more than 'out there,'" Colton went on. "He's *insane.*"

Chapter SEVEN

Scully was quiet as she and Mulder left the interrogation room and started out of the Baltimore Police headquarters. She had just made a choice. She could have worked with Colton and the Violent Crimes Section, a position any F.B.I. agent would respect. Instead she'd chosen to continue working with Mulder on the X-files. She hoped it was a decision she wouldn't regret.

"Mulder," Scully said as they walked through the busy headquarters. "Why'd you do that?"

"Do what?" Mulder asked innocently.

"After the lie-detector test," Scully reminded him, "you told Fuller and Colton that you thought Tooms committed the 1933 murders. You knew they'd never believe you. Why'd you push it?"

"Maybe I thought you caught the right guy," Mulder said.

Scully shook her head. By now she'd spent enough time with Mulder to know that was only half the answer. "And?" she prodded.

"Okay," Mulder continued. "*And* maybe I run up against so many people who are hostile just because they can't open their minds to the . . . possibilities that—"

"What?" Scully asked.

Mulder gave her one of his rare smiles. "That sometimes my need to mess with their heads outweighs my fear of looking like a fool."

"I think it was more than that," Scully said. "It seemed like you were acting very territorial."

"Of course I was," he said. "In our cases, you may not agree with what I hope to find, but at least you respect the journey. Colton only respects Colton. I guess that makes me want to keep him away from our investigation. And I don't mind him knowing that he's being kept out."

Scully paused a moment, surprised by Mulder's confession.

"But," Mulder went on calmly, "if you want to keep working with them, I won't hold it against you."

"Oh, no," Scully said, shaking her head. "You're not getting rid of me that easy. I know you must have something more than just the lie-detector test to back up this bizarre theory. And I want to see what it is."

The next day Scully knew exactly what Mulder had to back up his theory. She sat with him at a borrowed computer in the Baltimore police station. Mulder had called up Eugene Tooms's arrest report.

"Here," Mulder said, punching in a command on the keyboard, "are Tooms's fingerprints."

He punched some more buttons and the fingerprints enlarged, filling the screen.

Mulder entered another command. "Now this," he said as an elongated print appeared on the screen, "is the fingerprint I took from Usher's office. This print matches the old ones from the X-files. Here's the print from the 1933 murder at Powhatan Mill."

Scully didn't see the connection between Tooms's prints and the strange ones from the X-files. She glanced at Mulder and shrugged.

"Obviously, no match," he admitted. "But what if . . . somehow . . ." He punched in another command. Now Tooms's normal-looking human prints appeared only on the left half of the screen. The elongated prints appeared on the right half.

Working quickly, Mulder used the mouse to single out Tooms's middle left finger. He hit another button, and the computer stretched Tooms's fingerprint until it was as long and narrow as the one taken from Usher's office.

Scully's mouth dropped open as she saw what he was getting at.

"Just watch," Mulder said in a low voice. He ran the mouse across its pad, and the two images moved toward the center of the screen—until they overlapped and the computer beeped.

A small box flashed in the center of the screen. "Match 100%," it read. "Match 100%."

At first Scully's question stuck in her throat.

"How?" she asked at last. "How could Tooms's print be the same as a print taken from a murder committed over sixty years ago?"

"The only thing I know for certain," said Mulder, his eyes on the screen, "is that they let him go."

Chapter EIGHT

It was dark when Thomas Werner pulled into his driveway. He'd worked late at the office. Now he was ready for a drink and bed.

He reached for his briefcase and opened the car door. Then he stopped. Something felt different tonight. He sat for a moment, trying to pinpoint the feeling.

A cool autumn wind streamed through the open car door. Leaves rustled as they tumbled across the lawns, blew into the road, and scattered. During the day the streets of Werner's neighborhood rang with the sounds of children playing. But it was late now, and the neighborhood was quiet. It was so quiet that Werner could hear the wind in the trees and the *ping* under his car as the engine cooled. It was so quiet he could hear the sound of his own heartbeat.

Quiet wasn't a problem, Werner reminded himself. After all, he'd moved to this neighborhood because it was quiet.

He stepped out of his car. The sensor security light at the side of the house flashed on as he approached. It bathed the driveway in harsh white light. Werner glanced around, trying to shake the strange idea that something was wrong.

His three-story white house looked exactly the way it did every evening. Like his life, the house was neat, orderly, well kept. *Everything's fine,* Werner told himself. *You're imagining things.*

Werner walked up to the house, took out his keys, and let himself in through the side door.

Only pale moonlight lit the street. But the man who watched Werner leave his car and enter his house had no trouble seeing. His eyes glowed red with an inhuman fire.

Tooms crouched in the hedges on the other side of the street—waiting, watching. When Werner was inside his house, Tooms stood up. Moving swiftly, he crossed the street and went straight to Werner's house. Like an animal following a scent.

He stepped directly in front of the sensor light. It did not turn on.

Werner hadn't been imagining things. Something *was* wrong—terribly wrong. He was being hunted.

Methodically Tooms began to search for his point of entry. Keeping himself hidden in the bushes, he moved around the side of the house.

Werner's home was well protected. There were no windows or doors Tooms could use without setting off alarms.

Suddenly Tooms stopped. Before him, stretching up the side of the house, was a brick chimney. He'd found his way in.

Tooms reached up, grasping the bricks with the tips of his fingers. He began to pull himself up, as easily as a lizard scales a wall. He climbed slowly, surely, silently.

Tooms moved higher, past the first-floor windows. And then past the second-floor windows. He stretched out his fingers and reached for the edge of the roof. With uncanny strength, he lifted himself up onto the roof.

He gazed around in the darkness, and his eyes lit on the chimney stack. Now nothing could stop him. Thomas Werner didn't have a chance.

Werner stood in his kitchen. He loosened his tie and frowned as he began to read through his mail. More bills. More people asking for money. Then he stopped reading and looked up. He'd heard a noise—like a man grunting with effort. *No*, Werner told himself. *Couldn't be*. He took off his jacket and began to fix himself a drink.

On the roof Tooms peered down through the

chimney opening. It was narrow, no more than six inches by twelve. This one wouldn't be easy. He concentrated, sweat beading his forehead. Then he leaned over, stuck one arm deep into the chimney, and stretched. He stretched until the tiny bones in his fingers cracked from the strain. He stretched until his hand reached down three stories—and gripped the bricks at the very bottom of the flue.

Carefully Tooms lowered his head into the chimney. The rectangular space was even narrower than he'd thought. There was barely room for his head. He tried to wriggle his shoulders in, but they were way too wide.

With a sickening dull *pop,* Tooms dislocated his left shoulder from the socket. His shoulder slipped down into the opening. There was another *pop,* and the right shoulder followed. Tooms could smell Thomas Werner's sweat. Feel the heat of the blood in his veins. With every sense focused on his victim, what he had to do next was easy. Drawing on his incredible strength, Tooms began to squeeze himself down the narrow chimney.

Werner looked up a second time as he heard a *click* coming from the living room. Curious, he walked toward the noise. As always, everything in the living room was in its place.

Except the glass fireplace doors. They were slightly ajar. Wind whistled in from outside, and tiny flecks of ash blew onto the carpet.

Werner started to close the glass doors. Then he thought better of it and decided to light a fire. A fire would make the empty house seem cozy.

He took a log from the wood basket and threw it on the hearth. Then he knelt and lit the kindling from below. Seconds later a bright yellow fire began to flicker. Werner watched the tiny flames dance.

Quite suddenly the fire died. For a second Werner wondered if something was blocking the flue. He opened the matchbox, but it was empty. He stood up, sure there were more matches in one of the kitchen drawers. He turned toward the kitchen and stopped dead in his tracks.

Something was in the house—and it was rushing straight at him. It looked like a man, but it couldn't be. Whoever—or whatever—it was had eyes that blazed red fire.

Werner never even had a chance to scream. Moving swiftly, his attacker stuffed a gag into his mouth. Terrified, Werner tried to fight back. His struggles were useless. His attacker slammed him to the floor with unbelievable force. Werner's head hit hard. The fight was over.

Thomas Werner was unconscious when Eugene Tooms took what he had come for.

Chapter NINE

Thomas Werner had lived a solitary life. He'd rarely had visitors. But the next day his house was filled with people. All of them were cops, trying to reconstruct what had happened the night before. Somewhere in Werner's house there had to be a clue that would lead them to the murderer.

Baltimore Police Detective Johnson stretched out a metal tape measure. He gave the end to a uniformed officer. The officer held it at the tip of Werner's foot. Detective Johnson brought the tape to the wall behind Werner's head.

"Seventy-eight inches from the south wall," the detective announced. He snapped the tape back into its holder. As far as he could tell, the victim had died sometime the night before. And the body hadn't been moved after the death occurred. But this murder was every bit as mysterious as the ones before it. Once again there was no point of entry. Once again the victim's liver was gone.

Johnson turned as Tom Colton hurried into the house. The young F.B.I. agent looked stressed and frustrated.

"Let's run a check on liver transplants in the next twenty-four hours," Colton ordered. "Maybe this is black market. Someone who's making money selling livers to people who are desperate for a transplant."

Johnson was not impressed by this theory. In fact, he wasn't impressed by Colton. "Come on," he said impatiently. "You've got to be kidding."

"At this point, I'll give *any* theory a shot," Colton snapped. He ran a hand wearily through his hair. "Any sane theory, that is."

Colton looked even more stressed as Scully and Mulder passed the outside guard and entered the house.

Colton stepped toward them quickly. "I'm sorry, Dana," he said, "but I only want qualified members of the investigating team at the scene."

"What's the matter, Colton?" Mulder asked softly. "Are you worried that I'm going to solve your case?"

Mulder started toward the body. Colton reached out and grabbed his arm. Mulder remained calm, but he gave Colton a glance that let him know he had no authority to touch another agent. Colton let go of Mulder almost at once. Still, he continued to block his path.

Scully stepped between the two men. "Tom, we

have authorized access to this crime scene," she told her former classmate.

Neither Mulder nor Colton moved. It was definitely a standoff. Scully knew it was up to her to break it. Unfortunately Colton was every bit as stubborn as Mulder.

She had one weapon to use against Colton, the only thing he really cared about—his career. "Tom," she said in a firm voice, "a report of your obstructing another officer's investigation might stick out in your personnel file."

Colton's eyes flashed at her, and Scully knew their friendship was over. But he stepped aside to let Mulder examine the crime scene. Then Colton turned to Scully, his voice low and furious. "Tell me something, Dana," he said. "Whose side are you on?"

"The victim's," Scully told him.

She left Colton and went to see what the police officers had found so far.

On the other side of the room, Mulder stood watching the police taking measurements. They did their jobs efficiently, barely looking at the corpse in the center of all the activity.

Werner had died with an expression of unbearable terror on his face. Mulder made himself think of Werner as more than a body. He'd been a man, probably not all that different from the men in this room. A man who didn't deserve the death he'd gotten.

Mulder watched Johnson as he drew the tape from Werner's hand to the fireplace. Mulder's eyes widened as he saw something the detective missed—a smudge of ash above the hearth. And there was something disturbingly familiar in its long, narrow shape.

"Sixty-five inches from the fireplace," Johnson said in a bored tone. He snapped in the tape and started to make notes on a pad.

Mulder moved to the fireplace and knelt to examine the mark more carefully. It wasn't a clear print, but the resemblance to the other prints was strong. Mulder noticed another smudge of ash leading up to the mantel.

Curious, he examined the mantel. Most people filled their mantels with photographs or knick-knacks. Werner's mantel was bare, covered only with a fine layer of dust.

Mulder looked more closely. Maybe Werner's mantel hadn't been quite as bare as he'd thought. In the midst of all the dust was a perfectly clean ring. Some object had sat there, Mulder realized. An object that had been moved very recently.

Mulder turned from the hearth as Scully came

up to him. "The victim is Thomas Werner," she reported. "Single, fifty-two years old—"

"It was Tooms," Mulder cut her off. "And he took something from the mantel."

Chapter TEN

Mulder sat in front of a microfiche machine in the basement of the Baltimore Police station. Reels of film were stacked up next to the machine. Mulder's eyes were locked on the screen as old photographs and documents streaked past at lightning speed.

He stopped the machine with a *clack*. The screen displayed a typed form. The first line read, "1903 Census." The census, Mulder knew, would tell him exactly who had been living in Baltimore at that time.

Mulder advanced the screen through a few more pages of census forms. He leaned forward eagerly as he found what he was looking for. This copy of the census form had been filled out by hand. The old-fashioned writing read, "Eugene Victor Tooms." Mulder sat back in his chair, smiling with satisfaction. Finally the pieces of the puzzle were starting to fit together.

Behind Mulder the door to the room opened. Scully walked in, holding a pad with notes on it.

"Baltimore P.D. checked out Tooms's apartment,"

she reported. "The address was a cover. No one's ever lived there. *And* Tooms hasn't shown up for work since he was arrested."

"I found him," Mulder said.

Scully gave her partner a questioning look.

"How do we learn about the present?" Mulder asked. "We look to the past. That's where it all began—in 1903 on Exeter Street." He pointed to the screen.

Scully began to read the census form aloud. "'Eugene Victor Tooms. Date of birth: unknown. Residence: apartment one-oh-three, Sixty-six Exeter Street, Baltimore, Maryland. Occupation: Dog-catcher.'" *A profession similar to that of the current Tooms,* she thought.

"Now look at the address of that first murder in 1903," Mulder said.

Scully picked up the X-file and opened it to the photocopy of a police report written in 1903. "'Address of victim,'" she read. "'Sixty-six Exeter Street, apartment two-oh-three.'" Scully's blue eyes widened as she saw what Mulder was driving at. "He killed the guy above him!"

"Maybe the neighbor played the Victrola too loud," Mulder suggested.

Scully ignored his joke. "This Eugene Tooms must be our Tooms's great-grandfather," she said excitedly.

"What about the prints?" Mulder asked. "Remember, every fingerprint is unique. And the other prints in the X-file are all a perfect match."

"Genetics might explain a similar pattern," Scully said quickly.

Mulder shrugged, neither agreeing nor disagreeing.

"Genetics might also explain the sociopathic attitudes and behaviors," Scully went on. She was determined to find a rational, scientific explanation for these strange coincidences.

"How?" Mulder asked.

Scully thought back to the case studies she'd read when she was in medical school. "It begins with one family member who raises kids with sociopathic behavior," she explained.

"Little murderers," Mulder translated.

"Or criminals," Scully agreed. "Most often kids who are violent. At any rate, a family whose kids are seriously disturbed. Then if that offspring raises a child who's equally dangerous . . ."

Mulder gave her a blank look, then said, "So, what is this—the anti-Waltons?"

"Well, what do you think?" Scully asked. She was starting to feel frustrated, as she usually did when she tried to convince Mulder of something rational.

"I think what we have to do is track Eugene Tooms," Mulder answered. "There are four victims down and one to go this year. If we don't get him right now, the next chance we're going to get is in—"

"The year 2023," Scully calculated.

"And you're going to be head of the bureau by then," Mulder added without missing a beat. "So I think you have to go through the census. I'm going to plow through this century's marriage, birth, and death certificates. And . . ." His voice trailed off as he looked at the screen and realized what a monumental task he'd set for himself.

"And what?" Scully asked.

"And do you have any Dramamine on you?" Mulder asked weakly. He nodded toward the microfiche machine with a pained look. "'Cause these things make me sick."

Scully bit back a smile and went in search of another microfiche machine.

Mulder opened a small box and took out another roll of microfilm. Patiently he threaded it through the machine. Then he loosened his tie, rolled up his sleeves, and put on his reading glasses. It was going to be a very long morning.

Mulder and Scully scrolled through years of

information on the city of Baltimore. On their screens the years flew by . . . 1904 . . . 1909 . . . 1912. And for every year, the two F.B.I. agents scanned information on thousands of people. They were searching for something—anything—about Eugene Victor Tooms.

Hours later, Mulder sat back in his chair and took off his glasses. He rubbed the bridge of his nose. He was tired and bored and beginning to think that maybe this search wasn't such a good idea. Still, he knew he couldn't afford to feel discouraged. He forced himself to turn back to the machine and the endless records.

He felt a small tug of hope when Scully sat down next to him a short time later. "Find anything?" Mulder asked.

Scully looked every bit as tired as he felt. "Nope," she replied. "Eugene Tooms seems to have disappeared off the face of the earth. What did you find?"

"Never born. Never married. Never died," Mulder reported.

"At least in Baltimore County," Scully added.

Mulder sighed. Scully was right. What if Tooms had spent part of his life somewhere else? How would they ever track him?

"I did find one thing, though," Scully said.

"What?" Mulder asked.

Scully handed him a slip of paper. "It's the current address of the man who investigated the Powhatan Mill murders in 1933."

Chapter ELEVEN

Scully and Mulder walked through the recreation room of Baltimore's Lynne Acres Retirement Home. A group of residents was gathered around a TV, watching a game show. Most were in wheelchairs. Nearly all of them looked to be at least eighty years old. The whole building smelled of old age.

Scully glanced at the group, then quickly looked away. Places like this made her feel sad. Would they find a clue here to the case of Eugene Tooms? she wondered.

An attendant came up to them. "I just checked for you," she said. "Frank Briggs is upstairs in his apartment. Number seven ninety-three. He's expecting you."

"Thank you," Scully said.

Five minutes later she and Mulder stood in the seventh-floor hallway, in front of Briggs's apartment. The door was slightly ajar. Mulder knocked.

"Come on in!" called a hoarse voice from inside.

Scully led the way into a tiny studio apartment.

A double bed covered with an orange spread took up most of the room. A lamp and a cheap pendulum clock sat on a tall dresser in front of a window. The clock ticked loudly. The walls gave testimony to Briggs's career as a police officer. Scully noted a photograph of a police squad and a certificate of merit.

Frank Briggs sat in a wheelchair near a window. He had to be about eighty-five, Scully guessed. He was dressed casually in an open-necked yellow shirt that pulled tightly over his stomach. Scully studied the retired detective's face. He had white hair, a mustache, and the crooked, swollen nose of a man who'd been in more than one fight. Behind gold wire-rimmed glasses, his blue eyes were still sharp.

Briggs gestured to two armchairs at the foot of his bed. Scully and Mulder sat down.

"I've been waiting twenty-five years for you," Briggs said.

"Sir?" Scully asked.

"I called it quits in 1968," Briggs explained. "After forty-five years as a cop."

"Can you tell us about the 1933 killings in Powhatan Mill?" Mulder asked.

Briggs nodded. "I was a sheriff then . . ." he began. His voice trailed off, as if the subject was difficult for him to talk about.

Sixty years later, Scully thought, *and the old man still seemed overwhelmed by the memories.*

She listened as the clock ticked and Briggs sighed. He motioned for them to draw closer, and then he began talking in a low voice. He spoke in short sentences, as though he didn't have enough breath for long ones.

"Powhatan Mill was like nothing else," he said. "I'd seen my share of murders before that. Bloody ones too. But I could always go home, pitch a few baseballs to my kid, and never give it a second thought. You gotta be able to do that when you're a cop. You'd go crazy if you couldn't. Right?"

Scully nodded. What Briggs said was true. In police work, you had to be able to leave your job behind when you went home.

"But those murders in Powhatan Mill," Briggs went on. "When I walked into that room, my heart went cold. My hands went numb. I could feel . . . *it*. . . ."

"Feel *what*?" Mulder asked.

Scully watched as the old man blinked back tears and struggled to explain. "In 1945," he said, "just after World War Two ended, I first heard about the Nazi death camps. And I remembered that room in Powhatan Mill. And now when I see the Kurds and the Bosnians on television . . . that room is there!"

"I'm not sure I see the connection," Scully said.

The old man sighed. "What I saw in that room— it was as if all the horrible acts that people are capable of . . . somehow gave birth to some kind of human monster. And that room in Powhatan Mill held the evidence of what that monster could do. I saw the bodies he left behind."

Briggs looked away then, as if he was embarrassed by the emotion in his voice.

Scully put a hand on his arm. "It's all right," she said gently. "I think I understand how you felt."

Briggs took a deep breath and went on. "That's why I've been waiting for you," he said. "Because I knew *it* was never going to go away. And I've been waiting for it to come back." His eyes searched Mulder's face. "It's killed again, hasn't it?"

"Four times. So far," Mulder told him.

Briggs pointed to a trunk in the corner beside his bed. "There's a box in the trunk there," he said. "Get it out for me, will you, please?"

Mulder opened the trunk and lifted out an old cardboard box with reinforced corners. He set the box down on the bed and wheeled Briggs over to it. The retired police officer removed the lid, and Scully saw that the box was filled with thick folders.

Briggs waved his hand over the box. "This is all the evidence I've collected," he told the two agents. "Officially and unofficially. Have a look."

"Unofficially?" Scully asked as she and Mulder began to leaf through the folders.

Briggs coughed into his hand. "I knew the five murders in 1963 were by the same . . . person," he said. "The same one who'd killed in thirty-three. But by then the sheriff's department had me pushing papers. They said I was too old. Wouldn't let me near the case. But I kept my own kind of tabs on things anyway. I knew that someday there'd be someone who could use what I found."

Scully reached into the box and pulled out a glass jar. Inside it was a clear liquid that was probably formaldehyde. A chunk of red tissue floated in the liquid.

"A piece of a removed liver?" she guessed.

Briggs nodded. "Left at the crime scene. You know, livers weren't the only trophies he took."

"What do you mean?" Mulder asked.

"In each case, family members reported small personal effects missing," Briggs replied.

Mulder's eyes met Scully's. She knew they were both thinking of the object missing from Werner's mantel.

"A hairbrush from the Walters murder," Briggs continued. "A coffee mug from the Taylor murder—"

"Have you ever heard the name Eugene Victor Tooms?" Mulder asked, kneeling beside Briggs's wheelchair.

The old man stopped cold. "You know I have." He rummaged through the contents of the box and pulled out a bulky folder.

"When they wouldn't let me in on the case in sixty-three, I did some of my own work," he said proudly. "I took these surveillance pictures."

He began to flip through a pile of black-and-white glossy photographs. He handed a grainy one to Mulder. "Here you go," he said. "That's Tooms."

Mulder studied the photograph without comment and passed it on to Scully.

"Course that was Tooms thirty years ago," Briggs added.

Everything in the photo—the cars, the signs in the store window—looked old. Everything except Eugene Tooms. Briggs had caught him as he was stepping out of a van. Tooms was wearing a dog-catcher's uniform. He had the same short bangs. He wore the same startled boyish expression.

A chill went through Scully as she realized that in 1963 Tooms had looked *exactly* the way he did thirty years later. He hadn't aged a day.

Mulder picked up another photo.

"Now that," Briggs said, "is the apartment

where Tooms lived. It was located at . . . uh . . ."

"Sixty-six Exeter Street?" Mulder guessed.

"That's it," Briggs said, looking pleased. "Right there."

Mulder held out the photograph to Scully and she examined it more closely. The photograph showed a tall brick building, like a warehouse, on a narrow street. A sign on it read, PIERRE PARIS & SONS.

Scully recognized the building as the sort that had been built at the turn of the century. But in 1963 it had still been in decent shape.

Mulder held his hand out to Frank Briggs. "Thank you," he said. "You've been a tremendous help." He turned to Scully and said, "I think it's time you and I checked out Sixty-six Exeter Street."

Scully nodded, but something tightened in the pit of her stomach. They were getting closer to Tooms; she could sense it. And she couldn't help feeling afraid of what they would find.

Chapter TWELVE

Scully's hands were on the wheel. Her eyes were fixed on the traffic ahead of her. But her mind was back on the conversation they'd had at Lynne Acres Retirement Home.

"What did you think of Frank Briggs?" Scully asked Mulder. She turned onto a street that led to one of Baltimore's oldest sections. They were headed for the building in Frank's photograph—66 Exeter Street.

"I think it's too bad Briggs is retired," Mulder answered. "He was a good cop."

"I meant his theory," Scully said. "That Tooms is some kind of a monster. The very worst that humans are capable of, all concentrated in one man."

Mulder shrugged. "I don't know if Tooms is evil the way Hitler was evil," he said. "I'm not sure he thinks that way. Or if he thinks at all. Tooms may be more like an animal, killing to survive. But in either case, the results are the same. He's a brutal murderer who's got to be stopped."

Scully drove faster as the traffic thinned out.

There were no office buildings or stores in this part of the city. The streets were lined with warehouses and old factory buildings. Most of them looked deserted.

"Here it is," Scully said, making a sharp turn.

Exeter Street was narrow and dark. Tall buildings on either side blocked the daylight. Scully thought Exeter looked more like a dead-end alley than a street. She parked the car across from number 66.

"Quiet neighborhood," Mulder observed.

"You mean abandoned," Scully said.

Barrels of trash were piled outside the buildings. The street was covered with litter. The buildings looked as if no one had cared for them—or even used them—for years.

Number 66 was definitely the same building they'd seen in Frank Briggs's photograph. Scully recognized its red-brick face and the two shorter buildings beside it. But now the red brick was crumbling. The windows were boarded up. The sign that read PIERRE PARIS & SONS was badly faded. And graffiti covered the ground-floor wall.

Scully stared up the building. If Mulder and Briggs were right, this was where Eugene Victor Tooms had lived in 1903. And in 1963. Was he here now?

She drew her weapon and followed Mulder to the boarded-up entry. It was time to find out.

Scully stepped inside 66 Exeter Street and switched on her flashlight. Beside her, Mulder did the same.

They were in a narrow hallway. The inside of the building was completely dark. Dust motes floated in the beams of their flashlights. The place smelled of mildew and rot.

The two agents moved silently through the old building. Ahead of them, their flashlight beams crisscrossed in the darkness.

At the base of a wooden stairway Scully and Mulder exchanged a glance. They would try the upstairs apartments if they had to. But first they'd check out the ground floor.

Scully led the way down the hallway to the apartment where Eugene Tooms had lived.

"Here's one-oh-three," she said, stopping at a battered wooden door.

She turned the knob and pushed. The door swung open easily. Scully went in first. The floor-boards creaked beneath her feet.

It was just an old apartment. The windows were boarded up. A thin trickle of light leaked through the rotting wood. Except for some garbage on the floor, the room was empty. But Scully couldn't stop a look of horror from crossing her face.

Mulder nodded, understanding. "The old man is right," he said. "You can feel it."

Nothing in Scully's scientific training had prepared her for this. This was not the sort of phenomenon she normally believed in: that you could step inside an empty room and feel something terrible. A memory trapped in the walls, lingering in the air. But Briggs *was* right. Something horrific had happened here. And the feel of it was still in this room. As real as the gun she held in her hand.

Scully played the beam of her light along the walls. She was determined to concentrate on the physical. She wanted evidence she could touch. Proof that would hold up in court.

She noted that the brick outer wall showed through the ripped plasterboard. The paint peeled from the walls. A filthy ceramic sink stood beneath a rusted medicine cabinet with missing doors. A stained mattress leaned against a wall. But there was no sign of Tooms. Clearly it had been ages since anyone had lived in the apartment.

"There's nothing here," Scully said to Mulder. "Let's go."

But Mulder's interest was caught by the old

mattress. He held it away from the wall and shined his flashlight behind it. He let the mattress drop to the floor. "Check this out," he said.

Scully saw what had drawn his attention: a rough hole about four feet high, cut straight through the plasterboard. *Big enough,* Scully thought, *for a man to fit through.* She sent the beam of her flashlight straight down—and saw a ladder dropping into the darkness.

"What's down there?" Mulder asked.

"I don't know," Scully replied. She tucked her gun into the waistband of her pants. "Let's find out."

Without hesitating, Scully lowered herself onto the metal ladder. The pendant on her necklace swung out as she started to climb down.

Mulder was right behind her.

There were only about a dozen rungs before they reached the bottom. They were in a pitch-black area, even darker than the hallway above. Scully shined her light overhead. Heavy pipes crossed low ceiling joists. They were definitely in the building's basement.

It was chilly and damp. And it felt even worse than it had in the apartment. Scully fought back a shiver. She wasn't about to let Frank Briggs's theories—or her own imagination—get the best of her.

Carefully the two agents began to check out the dark basement. Finally Scully shook her head. "Nothing," she said, disappointed. "It's just an old coal cellar."

"What's that?" Mulder asked. He aimed his flashlight straight ahead. Something reflected the light to him.

Mulder walked toward the shiny object. "Somebody having a garage sale?" he said.

On a wooden crate sat a collection of objects: a pipe, a coffee mug, a glass cigarette lighter, an enamel box, a candy dish, a snow shaker with a model of the earth inside it.

Mulder knelt down to examine the collection. He picked up the cigarette lighter so that Scully could see its base. "This is the shape that was on Werner's mantel," he said.

Scully nodded, thinking of what Frank Briggs had told them about Tooms. "Briggs said he kept trophies."

"Does Tooms live in here?" Mulder wondered aloud.

Still kneeling, he sent the beam of his light across the coal cellar. The far wall, Scully saw, was mottled and damp.

"It looks like the wall's deteriorating," she said.

"No," Mulder said. "Somebody made it that way."

Before Scully could ask him what he meant, Mulder went over to examine the wall. Seconds later she was at his side. He was right, she saw. Someone had plastered an odd assortment of things against the wall. Greasy rags, torn strips of newspaper, and garbage were all stuck together to form a large mound. It stretched from ceiling to floor and wall to wall.

"It's a nest," Mulder said, his voice low with amazement.

Scully saw that the nest had been stuck together with an oozing greenish yellow substance. In the very center of the mound was a hole. "Look," she said, "this must be the opening. Think there's anything inside?"

As if to answer her question, Mulder gingerly reached inside the hole and touched it.

Scully was about to do the same—and then she realized what the oozing substance was.

"Oh, my God, Mulder." She tried not to gag, but she felt sick to her stomach. "It smells like . . . I think it's *bile*. Tooms must have taken it from his victims' livers."

"Oh," Mulder said. He sounded a little sick. "Do you think there's any way I can quickly get it off my finger without betraying my cool exterior?"

Scully didn't bother to answer.

Mulder hastily wiped his hand on the floor.

Then he stood up and examined the nest again. "I don't think this is where Tooms lives," he decided. His mind was working quickly, putting together a pattern that would explain the X-files on this case. "I think this is where Tooms . . . hibernates."

"Hibernates?" Scully echoed.

"Just listen," Mulder said. "What if some genetic mutation could allow a man to awaken every thirty years?"

"Mulder," Scully said. This time he'd gone completely over the edge. Not even *he* could believe such an absurd theory.

But Mulder was too excited by his idea to stop. "What if the five livers could provide sustenance for that period?" he went on. "What if they allowed him to regenerate the cells in his body so that he never aged? What if Tooms is a twentieth-century genetic mutant?"

Scully mulled that one over for about five seconds. Then she dismissed it. The trophies and nest were eerie. Still, they didn't come close to making such a wild theory possible. But this wasn't the time to argue about it. She and Mulder had something much more serious to worry about.

"In any case," she said, "Tooms isn't here now. But he's going to come back."

Mulder nodded. "We're going to need a surveillance team."

Scully gave him a wry smile. She knew that getting backup was not going to be easy. Colton had fought the X-files involvement from the start. He wouldn't be happy when she requested additional agents.

"That'll take some finagling," she told Mulder.

"I'll keep watch, then," he said. "You go downtown and see what you can finagle."

Scully nodded. She'd do what she could.

The two agents started out of the coal cellar. This time Mulder was in the lead. Scully suddenly stopped, with a sharp intake of breath. "Wait," she called. "I—"

Mulder spun around. "What is it?"

"I—I think I'm snagged on something," Scully said. She twisted a bit. Whatever had been caught was suddenly released. "It's okay," she called. "I got it."

She followed Mulder up the ladder and out of the coal cellar.

The coal cellar's ceiling was covered with pipes. If Scully had shined her flashlight directly above her, she might have seen a hand among the pipes. A hand that now held her necklace.

If she'd shined her light even higher, she would

have seen the fire-red eyes of Eugene Tooms. He'd been there all along. Now his eyes followed the agents as they left the cellar. His hand tightened on Scully's necklace. A trophy for each victim. Four victims down. One to go. He'd just found number five.

Chapter THIRTEEN

Mulder sat in his car, directly across from 66 Exeter Street. Even in broad daylight the old building looked eerie. As if it held secrets. As if the darkness inside could reach out into the city and spread until daylight itself was swallowed.

Mulder reached into his pocket, drew out a handkerchief, and wiped his fingers. For the third time. He knew it was silly, but he couldn't help it. He couldn't forget what it had felt like to touch the bile that lined Tooms's nest. He knew Tooms was no ordinary man. And part of Mulder couldn't help feeling that Tooms's evil infected everything he touched.

Mulder shifted restlessly in the car. He tried not to be impatient. Waiting was a necessary part of his job. But he didn't like it.

His eyes flashed to the rearview mirror as the back door of his car opened and a middle-aged man wearing a suit got in. Seconds later another man slid into the front seat. Mulder had been expecting them. They were agents Kennedy and Kramer, from the Violent Crimes Section.

Mulder glanced at his watch. "It's about time," he said.

Kramer rubbed the bald spot on his head. "So, who we lookin' for again?" he asked.

Mulder held up the arrest report and mug shot of Tooms. "Eugene Tooms," he told them. "He's unarmed, but consider him dangerous."

The two agents nodded. Both were thick-bodied men, older than Mulder. Both looked confident. As if they'd already sewn up the case.

"Scully and I will be back to relieve you in eight hours if Tooms doesn't show," Mulder promised. "Right here."

"You got it," Kennedy said. Then he added in an undertone, "Spooky."

Both agents laughed. Mulder hesitated for a moment. But his face showed no reaction. They could call him whatever they wanted. Names didn't bother him. What bothered him was the certainty that Eugene Tooms would kill again.

In a small office inside the Baltimore police headquarters, Scully checked her watch. It was nearly six thirty in the evening. And now she had a little more than two hours before she had to rejoin Mulder on the stakeout. She might as well go home for a while. The idea of a hot bath was too good to pass up. She felt dirty somehow, as if the air in Tooms's coal cellar still clung to her skin.

She was putting the last of her things in her briefcase when the door to the office opened. Tom Colton swept in. He closed the door so hard that its frosted-glass window rattled.

Scully raised one eyebrow. Colton was definitely upset about something. He'd never been good at hiding his emotions.

Colton tossed a piece of paper onto the desk. "We have to talk," he said angrily.

Scully had a good idea what this was about. And the last thing she wanted to do was discuss it with Tom Colton. "I can't talk now," she said. "I have to meet Mulder."

"That's what we have to talk about," Colton insisted. He leaned forward and pounded on the desk as he spoke. "You're using two of my men to sit in front of a building that's been condemned for ten years," he said.

"It's not in any way interfering with your investigation," Scully told him calmly.

Colton's eyes hardened. "When we first had lunch, I really looked forward to working with you," he said. "You were a good agent, Dana. But now, after seeing the way you've been brainwashed by Mulder . . . I couldn't have you far enough away."

Scully stood up. She'd heard enough. Colton was acting like a spoiled three-year-old. Without looking at him, she started out of the office.

But Colton stopped her with a parting shot. "Don't bother going down there," he said. "I had the stakeout called off."

Scully whirled around to face him, her own temper finally snapping. "You can't do that!" she told him.

Colton smiled smugly. "You're right. I can't. But my regional supervisor can. Especially after I told him about the irresponsible waste of man-hours."

Scully moved toward the phone, but Colton grabbed it first.

"No, let me," he said with exaggerated politeness. "Let me call Mulder and tell him the news."

Scully shook with anger as Colton dialed. They were so close to catching Tooms. And Colton, with his overblown ego and ambition, was ruining it all.

"Is this what it takes to 'climb the ladder'?" she asked in a low, furious voice.

"All the way to the top," Colton assured her.

"Then I can't wait till you fall off and land on your face!" Scully told him.

Colton watched Dana storm out. He was smiling. He'd get Mulder and Scully off this case, once and for all.

He listened as Mulder's answering machine

picked up. "This is Fox Mulder," the recorded voice said. "I'm not here. Please leave a message."

It will be a pleasure, Colton thought as he waited for the tone. *It will be a pleasure to tell you that your stakeout has been canceled.*

Scully was distracted as she drove home. Her mind circled the case as if it were a solid wall and somehow she could find a way through. Her thoughts went back to Briggs. She remembered his talking about how he could usually forget a case when he went home. How that was necessary if you were going to do police work and not go crazy.

Scully knew exactly what he meant. Just the sight of the beautiful old building where she lived usually put the stress of work behind her. Tonight, though, that was impossible. This case stayed with her, every second of the day.

Scully parked in front of her building and walked toward the lit entryway. What she couldn't know was that this case really *had* come home with her.

Eugene Tooms hid behind the car that was parked in front of hers, watching her every move.

Chapter FOURTEEN

Darkness cloaked the city. Rush hour was nearly over. The downtown sidewalks were empty. Mulder found himself returning to 66 Exeter Street. He'd been restless all day. He hadn't been able to eat or sleep. He hadn't been able to get any work done in his office. He wasn't due to start his next shift on the stakeout for nearly two hours, but he couldn't stay away. Not when they'd found Tooms's nest. Not when they were so close to catching him.

He turned onto Exeter and parked across from number 66. There were no streetlights here. The shadow of the building loomed tall and menacing in the moonlight. Steam rose from a vent in the sidewalk. The street seemed even more deserted than it had during the day.

The street shouldn't be deserted at all, Mulder realized. He checked his watch. Kennedy and Kramer should still be here, watching the building.

Mulder got out of his car and scanned the empty street. There was no sign of the two agents. Or even of their car.

"Where is everyone?" he asked aloud. "Kramer, Kennedy?"

There was no answer.

"Scully," he said, "are you here?"

Again silence was his only answer.

Mulder had a bad feeling about this. Something was wrong. Very wrong.

He began running toward the building where Eugene Tooms lived.

Scully let herself into her apartment. She'd moved here just after she graduated from the Academy, and she'd worked hard at making it the perfect place to come home to. The airy rooms were decorated in warm, sunny colors. Everything was neat and clean and in its proper place.

Tonight, though, Scully paid no attention to what her apartment looked like. Moving with quick, angry motions, she hung up her coat and kicked off her shoes. She was still steaming about Colton's calling off the stakeout. She wondered what he'd said to Mulder, and how Mulder was taking it.

She poured herself a glass of sparkling water and picked up her cordless phone.

She punched in Mulder's number, then sighed as his answering machine played its message. Why was it that Mulder was never home when she really needed to talk to him?

"Mulder," she began. "I guess you went out since Colton gave us the night off. I say we file a complaint against him. I'm *furious*. Call me when you get in. 'Bye."

She hung up the phone and went to run her bath. She loved the big old claw-footed tub and the colorful tiles on the bathroom walls. Above the tub she'd hung loofahs and little shelves filled with bath oils. A tall frosted window flooded the room with light during the day. At night the bright tiles made the room seem cozy.

Scully turned on the hot and cold taps, adjusting them until the water was the right temperature. She wished Mulder would call back. She couldn't really relax until she talked to him. Until they figured out how to get around Colton. And capture Tooms.

She was about to pin up her hair when she realized that her hairbrush was in her purse. And her purse was in her bedroom. She went into the bedroom to get the brush.

That was why she didn't see the outline of a man's body pressed against her bathroom window.

Mulder pushed through the broken door of 66

Exeter Street. He couldn't understand what had happened to the two F.B.I. agents who were supposed to be on the stakeout. And he couldn't forget that Tooms had killed once before in this building. Mulder just hoped he hadn't killed here again.

He snapped on his flashlight and made his way down the deserted hallway to apartment 103. The door was still open.

As soon as Mulder stepped into the empty apartment, his heart began to race. He had never been so sure that Evil was a living, breathing presence. And he had just stepped into its lair. There was no doubt in his mind. Tooms had been back.

Mulder wanted nothing more than to run as far and fast as he could. But he forced himself to go forward. Even if it meant meeting Eugene Tooms.

The old mattress was exactly where he and Scully had left it. Holding his flashlight with one hand, Mulder drew his gun with the other. Slowly he stepped through the hole in the wall. Then he inched down the ladder into the coal cellar.

He shined his light around the dark space. The basement too looked untouched. It didn't make sense, Mulder told himself. Tooms must have come back; he could feel it.

His heart pounding, Mulder crossed the basement floor. He cast the beam of his flashlight onto the wooden crate. Tooms's trophies shined back at him. Mulder recognized the snow globe and the pipe and Werner's lighter.

But this time there was a new trophy too. One that sent ice water through Mulder's veins. Dangling from the trophy crate was Scully's necklace.

Chapter FIFTEEN

Scully stood in her bedroom, facing her mirror. She was pinning up her hair for her bath, but she barely saw her own reflection. Her mind was still on the case. She knew they'd gotten closer to finding Tooms today. And what they'd found made her very uneasy. *Could Mulder possibly be right?* she wondered. *Was Tooms some sort of mutant who hibernated for thirty years at a stretch? And then kept himself alive by murdering people and eating their livers? Had he really been alive since the beginning of the century? Or earlier?*

Smiling ruefully, Scully shook her head. Until she saw medical tests that proved otherwise, she'd deal with Eugene Victor Tooms as a human. A very dangerous human.

Scully glanced at her watch. If she took her bath, that would give Mulder another hour or so to call back. After her bath, whether or not she had heard from him, she'd head over to Exeter Street. Even if Mulder didn't check his phone messages, she was sure he would meet her there. And if they had to finish the stakeout on their own, they would.

She wasn't about to let Colton blow this case.

She went back into the bathroom just in time to shut off the water. The tub was nearly full. She reached over to one of the shelves that held her bath oils and lotions. She chose a bottle of clear blue liquid and poured it into the steaming tub. The smell of rosemary filled the room.

Scully started to undo the bottom button on her shirt. But she stopped as she realized she'd forgotten to bring in her robe from the bedroom. The case definitely had her distracted, she told herself. Either that or her mind was going. She headed back toward the bedroom.

That was when she felt it. Something damp on her wrist. She held it up to the light and saw two drops of clear greenish yellow liquid.

It didn't make sense, she thought. The bath oil was blue. And besides, she hadn't spilled any. She thought for a second. The building was an old one. Maybe there was a leak in the ceiling from the apartment above her.

She looked up at the ceiling and felt the muscles in her chest tighten with fear. Directly above her was a heating grate. A thick greenish yellow liquid was pooling in the corner of the grate.

No, Scully thought. She fought down a surge of panic. She lifted her hand and sniffed the fluid on her wrist. Her body froze with terror as she recognized the smell.

She was suddenly horribly aware of how alone she was. And of how many hiding places there were in her apartment. Especially for someone who could squeeze himself inside a pipe. Or under a counter. Or into the air vent above her.

She touched the greenish yellow substance. She had to be sure. And she was. There was no mistaking it. It could only be bile from a human liver.

"Oh, my God," she said softly.

Mulder sat in his car and glared at the flashing red and blue lights in the distance. He rested one elbow on the steering wheel and held his head in his hand. He couldn't believe it. Of all the times for an accident to happen on the highway! For the past twenty minutes traffic hadn't moved.

All Mulder could think of was what he'd found in the basement of 66 Exeter Street. *Tooms has her necklace. Tooms has Scully's necklace.* That could mean only one thing: Scully was going to be the fifth victim.

Mulder reached for his cellular phone and punched in Scully's number. For the twentieth time. He'd been calling her since he'd left Exeter Street.

Once again Scully's phone rang and rang and

rang. Mulder couldn't understand it. Scully had an answering machine. The machine should be picking up if she wasn't home.

"Come on, Scully," he muttered. "Answer!"

But all he heard was the sound of her phone ringing endlessly. Somehow this scared him even more than seeing her necklace in Tooms's lair.

Mulder sighed with relief as the flashing lights began to move. A few seconds later the cars ahead of him started to roll forward again.

Mulder tried Scully's number one last time while he waited for traffic to resume its normal speed. Then he threw down the phone and hit the gas pedal hard. He hoped he wasn't too late. He hoped there was some nice, innocent reason that Scully wasn't answering her phone.

There was, in fact, a reason that Scully wasn't answering. But it wasn't nice or innocent. She didn't answer because her phone never rang. Mulder wouldn't get through no matter how many times he tried. No one could. Because in the basement of her building, someone had cut the wires to Scully's phone.

For a second, panic froze every muscle in Scully's body. *I'm alone in the apartment with Tooms.* Her heart hammered a rhythm of terror through her veins. *Tooms is hunting me.*

She ordered herself to take a deep breath. The panic broke and instinct took over. She raced for the bedroom. Her gun. She had to get her gun.

She'd left only one light on in the room—the lamp on her bedside table. The rest of the bedroom was dark. Tooms could be anywhere. In her closet. Under the bed. Crouching in the shadows. *Please,* she thought, *don't let him be in here.*

She made it to her desk. The desk was in the darkest part of the room. Frantically she searched for the gun. Her hand closed on papers, her laptop, a box of paper clips. The gun wasn't there.

She forced herself to think calmly. Where had she left it? She knew she'd brought the gun home from work. In her bag. The gun was still in her bag. And the bag was on the bed.

She dashed across the room. She reached for her bag and yanked it open. Her heart slowed as her fingers closed on the familiar metal barrel.

Now *she* was the hunter.

She braced the gun with both hands straight in front of her. Slowly she began to move through the apartment, searching for Tooms.

Using her shoulder, Scully turned on the light in the bedroom. She looked under the bed, in the closet, under the desk, anywhere he might be. But she was the only one in the bedroom. Tooms was still in the apartment, she was sure of it. And he was hiding.

Carefully she made her way into the living room. Remembering the prints in Werner's house, she checked the fireplace. No sign of Tooms. Was he still in the air vent above the bathroom?

She edged into the hallway that led to the bathroom. She moved slowly, soundlessly. She felt as if she were listening with her entire body—waiting for Tooms to make the slightest noise.

She glanced up at an air vent in the hall ceiling. Nothing. She whirled as she thought she heard a noise behind her. Deliberately she trained her weapon on a heating grille just above the floor. Nothing again.

She took another deep breath and turned back toward the bath.

She didn't see the cover of the heating grille opening. She only heard the ear-splitting *crack* as it flew off the wall and hit the hardwood floor.

Instantly Tooms's hand shot out of the vent and locked around her leg, pulling it out from under her.

Scully hit the floor hard. The gun flew out of her hand and skittered out of reach, across the bathroom floor and under the tub.

She managed to twist around so that she was on her back. Terror paralyzed her as she stared at

Tooms. His face was framed by the rectangular air vent. He no longer looked scared and innocent. He looked like a vicious predator about to devour its prey.

For a long moment Scully and Tooms locked stares. Then a low, animal growl filled the apartment. And Tooms, using unbelievable strength, began to pull her toward him.

Scully knew that she'd never been up against anything like Tooms. That this would be the hardest fight of her life. And that if she didn't win, it would be the last.

Chapter SIXTEEN

Mulder's car came to a screeching stop in front of Scully's apartment building. He got out of the car and stood for a moment. His eyes scanned the fourth-floor windows. There was a light on in Scully's apartment. She was there, all right. And he'd bet everything he owned that Tooms was there with her.

Mulder raced into the entrance of the building, then cut through the lobby to the stairway. He wasn't about to risk getting stuck in the elevator.

He took the stairs two at a time. Then he raced down the hallway that led to Scully's apartment.

"Scully!" He banged on the door.

There was no answer.

"Scully!"

Still no answer. He tried the knob. Scully had been careful, as usual. The door was tightly locked.

Mulder put his ear to the door. There were sounds coming from inside the apartment, as though some sort of struggle was going on.

At least she's still alive, Mulder told himself. But he knew that unless he got in there fast, Scully had only a few minutes left to live.

☠   ☠   ☠

Scully knew she had to do two things. She had to get out of Tooms's grasp. And she had to get her gun back. Otherwise she didn't stand a chance.

Desperately she caught hold of the bathroom door frame. Using all her strength, she pulled herself toward it. At the same time she kicked furiously at the arm that held her ankle. She kicked again. This time she managed to wrestle free of Tooms's grip.

Still on her back, she slid away from the duct and into the bathroom. She paused for a second, terrified and breathless. Then she watched with disbelief as Tooms's body stretched—impossibly long and impossibly narrow—and shot out of the air duct. Scully never even had time to scream. One second he was in the air. The next he'd landed on top of her, pinning her to the ground.

Scully struggled fiercely to escape, but Tooms was too strong for her. He was on his knees, straddling her. He held her down with the strength of ten. He stank of sweat and bile.

Scully wrenched her body to the side, trying to throw him off her. Tooms didn't budge. He grabbed her chin with one hand. Then he lifted his other hand. She knew what he was planning. He was going to hit her and knock her out—so that he could take what he wanted without a fight.

Scully didn't know if she had enough strength to escape him. But she definitely had enough to make things difficult. Before he could hit her, she landed a hard uppercut on his jaw. Tooms's head snapped back, and Scully felt a flash of hope. At least he could be hurt.

Tooms drew back his arm again. This time Scully reached up with both hands. Like a cat, she went for his eyes with her nails. Scratching, gouging. If she could blind him, she'd have a chance.

With a cry of rage, Tooms grabbed her wrists. She gasped as he slammed them to the floor above her head. With one hand he pinned them there.

And with the other he reached for her right side. His eyes burned fire red with hunger.

Scully's heart was pounding so fast she thought it would explode. Terror flashed through her like sheet lightning. This was it. She knew exactly what was going to happen. The same thing that had happened to George Usher and Thomas Werner. Tooms was going to kill her—so that he could live and kill again.

And she was helpless to stop him.

Chapter SEVENTEEN

Mulder kicked at Scully's door. His leg ached from ankle to thigh. It figured that Scully would choose an apartment with a door like iron.

He drew back his leg and sent another powerful blow into the wood. Finally it began to splinter. He kicked again—and this time the door gave way.

Mulder let himself into the darkened apartment and drew his gun. "Scully, are you in here?" he shouted.

A muffled cry was his answer.

He threw on the living room light switch. The room was neat, perfect, empty.

"Scully?"

He heard muffled sounds again. This time he was sure they were coming from the bathroom.

Mulder reached the open bathroom door, and for a second he didn't even notice Tooms. All he saw was that Scully was still alive.

Then Mulder's brain quickly made sense of the scene. Tooms had released her. He stood with his face to the bathroom window. A shattering sound filled the room as Tooms's bare fist smashed through the frosted glass. With inhuman strength, Tooms stretched his hand up and began to lift himself toward the opening in the glass.

But Scully was up. And she wasn't about to let Tooms escape. She tackled him hard, grabbing his legs.

"Freeze!" Mulder shouted. But he couldn't shoot. Scully was in the way.

Mulder's heart sank as Tooms turned on Scully.

He grabbed her throat and pushed her backward. Mulder had a good idea how strong Tooms was. Scully was about two seconds away from having her neck snapped.

Quickly Mulder opened his handcuffs and went after Tooms. He grabbed Tooms's arm, but he wasn't fast enough to cuff him.

Tooms let go of Scully and whirled to face Mulder. Like an enraged bull, Tooms charged, knocking Mulder to the floor.

Mulder rolled, then kicked at Tooms. It didn't stop Tooms, but it bought Mulder a little time and distance. He knew that if Tooms actually got hold of him, he wouldn't have a chance.

Tooms stood over him now, roaring like a wounded animal. He raised his hand like a knife edge, about to drive it into Mulder.

Scully grabbed Tooms's other arm. She snapped

Mulder's open handcuff around Tooms's wrist and fastened the other cuff to the bathtub faucet.

Instantly Mulder was up, his automatic trained on Tooms. Tooms jerked at the metal cuff. He twisted and pulled. But the old fixtures were strong. And gradually Tooms settled down. This time he couldn't escape.

With his gun on Tooms, Mulder glanced at Scully. She was leaning against the wall, still breathing hard. "You all right?" Mulder asked her.

Scully nodded. She was trembling and she looked exhausted.

Mulder glanced back at their prisoner. "Well, at least he's not going to get this year's quota."

Scully smiled, for the first time all day.

Chapter EIGHTEEN

Morning sunlight streamed through the windows of the Lynne Acres Retirement Home. Frank Briggs sat in his apartment, reading the daily paper. He was in his wheelchair and alone, as usual. There was no longer much he could do to change the news, he reflected. But at least he could still keep up with it.

A heavy sadness filled him as he saw the front-page headline. It read, THE CONSEQUENCES OF ETHNIC CLEANSING. Above the headline was a photograph of war casualties. *It was horrifying,* Briggs thought. *Even worse, it was endless. Why did men keep doing these things to each other?*

Shaking his head in sorrow, Briggs turned the page. His eyebrows rose in surprise as he caught sight of a much smaller headline: SUSPECT CAUGHT IN SERIAL KILLINGS. And right next to it was Eugene Victor Tooms's mug shot.

Briggs blinked back tears as he read the story. Those two F.B.I. agents, Mulder and Scully, had done it. They'd put that monster Tooms behind bars. A case he had started on in 1933 was finally closed.

Briggs sighed, allowing himself a rare moment of contentment. Finally he'd done his part to stop a little of the horror.

In a tiny cell in the Maryland State psychiatric ward, Eugene Tooms sat on the narrow prison bed. He was holding the same newspaper Briggs held. For a moment his eyes rested on his own mug shot. Then, methodically, he began to rip the paper into long, narrow strips.

Tooms lifted one of the strips and ran his tongue across it. He crumpled the slimy paper in his hand. Then he tossed it at the wall in the corner of his cell. It slid to the floor—at the base of a growing mound of shredded papers. Tooms picked up another strip of paper and ran it along his tongue. He gazed at the corner with contentment. It looked a lot like the wall in the basement of 66 Exeter Street.

Mulder stood outside the door to Tooms's cell and stared through the small circular observation window. He knew that the door was made of steel. And that the barred cell was reinforced by a strong chain link. Tooms was safely imprisoned. So why did he still seem so scary?

Mulder watched as Tooms methodically shredded the newspaper and added the pieces to the pile on the wall. Mulder didn't look away even when he heard Scully's footsteps coming toward him from the other end of the corridor.

"Look at him," Mulder said in a troubled voice. "He's building another nest."

Just the sight of Tooms made Scully's skin crawl. His building a new nest was not a good sign. Still, he was in custody. Finally.

"Everything's been filed," she reported. "They've got our statements. The evidence has been tagged. We can turn the investigation over to the Baltimore Bureau now."

Mulder didn't respond.

"Colton actually tried to worm in on the case," Scully continued. "But his superiors caught on. He's been bumped off the Violent Crimes Section." She tried to keep the triumph out of her voice as she added, "They reassigned him to the White-Collar Crime section at the Sioux Falls Bureau."

Mulder shrugged. Colton didn't matter to him. And he never had.

"You'll be interested to know, I've ordered some genetic tests on Tooms," Scully went on. "The preliminary medical exam revealed quite abnormal development in the muscular and skeletal systems."

Mulder gave her a faint smile. "I didn't need the results of a medical exam to tell me that."

Scully ignored his comment and continued. "Tooms also has a continually declining metabolic rate. His body's metabolism dips way below the levels registered in deep sleep." She hesitated. "Did you hear what I said, Mulder?"

Inside the cell, Tooms tore another strip of paper and ran his tongue over it.

"I heard you," Mulder said, his voice weary. "It's just that I'm thinking about all these people putting bars on their windows. Spending good money on high-tech security systems and trying to feel safe. And I look at this guy, and I think—it's not enough. None of it is enough."

Scully put a hand on Mulder's shoulder. "Come on," she said gently. "It's time to go."

Eugene Tooms was only barely aware of Mulder and Scully's leaving. He tore another strip of paper, wet it with his saliva, and added it to his nest. He paused as he heard footsteps on the other side of his cell door.

A narrow slot in the door opened. A guard slid a food tray into the slot.

Tooms got up and took the tray. He sat back down on his bed. He didn't bother with the food. He'd already fed on what he needed to stay alive.

His eyes were fixed on the cell door. The guard

had left the panel open so that Tooms could put the tray back when he was done eating.

Tooms listened to the guard's footsteps dying away.

His eyes glowed red as he gazed at the light pouring through the narrow slot. A smile crossed Tooms's face. It was a very narrow opening. Maybe only six inches high and nine inches wide. But that really wasn't a problem if you knew how to squeeze. . . .